Twelve Years of Christmas

a.k.a.

The Trials and Tribulations of an Overworked Toy Maker

written and illustrated by

KUBER KAUSHIK

Twelve Years of Christmas a.k.a. The Trials and Tribulation of an Overworked Toy Maker

Written, Illustrated, and Edited by Kuber Kaushik

Copyright © 2020 Kuber Kaushik

Cover design by Kuber Kaushik and Aditya Vishwanath

ISBN 979-8-58-418192-5

First Edition, 2020

Dedication

Table of Contents

Author's Note..v

TWELVE YEARS OF CHRISTMAS

2008 - Credit-Crunched Christmas 1

2009 - The Missing Reindeer 6

2010 - Midsummer's Mail 12

2011 - Mechanical Difficulties 17

2012 - The Rant Before Christmas 25

2013 - The Accident Before Christmas 32

2014 - Reindeer Escape 37

2015 - An Invisible Christmas 45

2016 - The Surrender of Santa 53

2017 - The Tale of Whitebeard... 62

2018 - The Noel Conspiracy 72

2019 - A Social Reindeer Story 83

Epilogue: 2020 - The Once and Future Claus 91

About the Author.. 94

Author's Note

I have at times wondered why I am drawn to the Christmas season, and have come to the conclusion that there are many reasons. I have fond memories of this time of the year. It occurs around the solstice when the nights are long, which is a delight for nocturnal creatures such as myself.

To address what some who know me might wonder – Christmas holds no religious significance for me. My general views on such matters range from agnostic to dystheistic and atheistic to antitheistic, so let's leave that alone for now.

Suffice to say, the story of the season is what draws me in. That is to say – the story of celebration in winter's heart. A time of food, music, and laughter. And also, a time of kindness. Holidays like these are a reason to be kind. I wish that we didn't need a reason (and there are definitely exceptional people who don't), but given the unrelenting pace of everyday life, it has been my observation and experience that sometimes we do need an excuse to take a breath and embrace empathy.

I've also always preferred 'Merry' to 'Happy' as a seasonal greeting. Merriment and laughter are sometimes easier than real joy. For that reason, I've always wanted to help people laugh at this time of the year, and for the last dozen years or so, these amateurish poems have done just that.

I hope you enjoy reading them, and a Merry Winter's Solstice to all.

Twelve Years of Christmas

a.k.a.

The Trials and Tribulations of an Overworked Toy Maker

Credit-Crunched Christmas

'T was a month or three before Christmas,

And events had risen to a dangerous boil,

Santa's workshop was in complete disarray,

As chaos side-tracked the labour and toil.

"Taxes on the rise,

Wages are getting low,"

Santa muttered grimly,

And indeed things were so.

"The Economy is in tatters,

And with a capital E at that,

And I'm in a great fix,

As sure as I am fat!

The Elves union is on the warpath,

Demanding insurance and leisure,

They want off-days, and sick-days,

And compensation for seizures!

I blame that Harry Potter woman,

For giving them the information.

Three years ago they were happy

With just proper ventilation.

And even faithful Rudolph,

Wants health-insurance benefits.

So what could I do but say,

Yes - I'll put it on my list.

He deserves it though, poor reindeer,

Lately, he's been trembling like a goose,

Hasn't been the same since that governor

Mistook him for a moose.

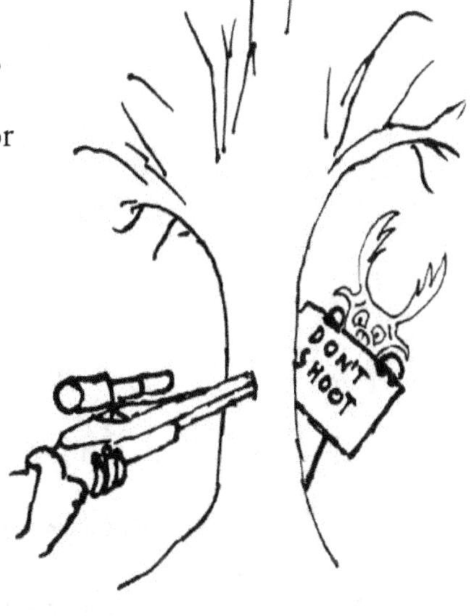

But worst oh worst of all these griefs,

Is the housing market, oh yes, indeed!

I've been searching for a new estate,

For many a week to avoid an ugly fate.

No loans for a toy-manufacturer these days,

Is all that I hear,

Even if it means a budgeted Christmas

This very year.

Yet I try and explain, to little avail,

Clearly and concisely to those who might hear,

That the Economy in crisis, does but pale,

To the problem that is the main issue to fear.

It's global warming,

Look it up if you please,

It means more water,

Far less Christmas trees.

So under pressure of C02,

Sulfur dioxides, and the Sun,

Come summer, 2010, my workshop

Will be melted and gone!"

Finishing muttering thus

To his heart's content,

Santa sighed deep

And went off to bed.

Mayhap Christmas time would send a miracle,

To keep the fat man afloat.

A house loan, a tax exemption,

Or maybe just a house-boat.

2 0 0 9

The Missing Reindeer

'Twas five days and a half before Christmas

When the Reindeers all vanished.

Suddenly ran AWOL, underground,

Without a word, as if banished.

"By my beard and my belly!"

Echoed Santa, beside himself with rage.

"Such shocking behaviour!

They should really all act their age!

I knew Rudolph was trouble,

But what in the world could I say?

His bright shiny nose,

Did once, indeed, save the day."

Grumbling and mumbling

About the mysteriously missing herd,

He strapped on his snowshoes,

And set off without another word.

Whether he liked it or not

It was not he who flew through the night,

But rather the reindeer

Who pulled the sleigh on its long flight.

He searched in the tundra's mists,

And beyond the glacier's reach,

To tropical forests, urban zoos,

And even on a bright southern beach.

He asked the Yeti, the Easter Bunny

The Sandman and the Prince of Thieves,

But none had seen the straying deer,

Not a hair or hoof, or even a sneeze.

Finally, Santa threw in the towel,

And swallowed his brimming pride.

He called the RSPCA,

And imagine what he was to find.

The reindeer had run all the way to PETA,

Much to Santa's surprise,

And were now settled in a national park,

Far away from prying eyes.

After much paperwork, strife,

And bellowing about limited time,

Visitation rights were granted,

As the dawn of Christmas Eve did chime.

"What in the world is all this about?"

Shouted Santa at Donner, who munched on a leaf,

"We've had this argument before,

After that incident where we crashed on a reef!

Compensation, Treats, a Pension and Sick-Leave.

The polar bears arbitrated this whole deal.

We had an agreement, a binding contract,

Signed with a snowflake shaped seal!"

Then said Blitzen to Santa, much ashamed,

"Do apologize, dear boy, but we've had a bit of a scare,

Rudolph learned that we were tracked,

By radar and satellite every time we take to the air.

And there's this whole new issue that's come up,

It's all on the Internet, you see,

Some strange militant group called NORAD

Intends to greet us with F-15s!

They'll probably blast us out of the sky

Without any questions cast,

And we know you don't have permissions

Because you've never asked.

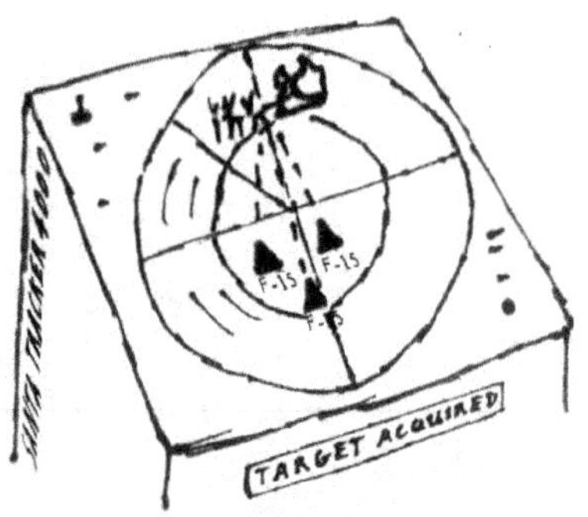

So we're not coming back

Without a few definite guarantees.

Maybe equip the sleigh

With flares and some enchanted shields."

At this Santa simply scratched his head,

And could only see a single thought to find,

That his neurotic hooved helpers

Had completely lost their collective mind.

He'd have to find a replacement

That was the only thing to do.

Some elk, a few moose,

Perhaps an arctic wolf or two.

So this year, kids around the world,

Look to the skies as night unfurls,

Waiting with bated breath to see featured

The next generation of sleigh-pulling creatures.

2 0 1 0

Midsummer's Mail

'T was six months and half before Christmas,

And Santa was on a well-deserved break,

Lying on a sunny, sandy, white beach,

Sipping a rainbow coloured milk-shake.

Quietly idyllic as this sounds though,

Dark storm clouds were in the air.

Because little did the world know that

The jolly old man was in despair.

He was taking this opportunity

To catch up on his overdue mail.

Electronic, paper and every other kind,

Each letter to be read without fail.

They were sorted neatly into four types,

Letters, bills, junk mail, and complaints.

Each type required a different approach.

And the unwavering patience of a saint.

Health and safety inspectors had found

That his workshop was floating on thin ice,

Had got in touch with the Elves' Union,

And got them to go off on one of their strikes.

"It'll be the fifth time this century,"

Muttered Santa with a dark brooding frown.

"If this happens much more often,

I won't have much choice but to shut down."

His accountant too had sent him a message,

Declaring that his finances were in disrepair.

"Making toys just doesn't cost the same," it said

"As when you started this whole Christmas affair.

I thus urge you to give some serious thought

To charging for deliveries or at the least

Register your likeness as a creative property

Used on street-corners, books, cards, and movies.

The royalties alone will cover the next century's costs,

And don't get me started on the merchandising rights...

If you left it to me, Saint Nicholas,

I could make you a millionaire overnight."

Rudolph had sent a colourful post-card,

From a vetenarian's hospital in the USA.

"Having the shining nose problem fixed,

Get new fog lights for the sleigh."

In other events, his elven legal team

Had delivered a file with some apprehension,

(They too were on strike, but this news

Just couldn't wait till Santa's concession.)

Fifteen arrest warrants had been issued,

From thirteen different parts of the world

Breaking and entering, violating air-safety,

And accidentally ramming an endangered bird.

With all this hovering gloomily over his head,

Santa sighed and looked at the mail that remained.

And then brightened as he started on the letters,

Old-fashioned, traditional and modestly restrained,

Christmas wishlists from all across the world.

Some six months and a half too early maybe

But this didn't bother him, not at all.

A break at last from all the bureaucracy.

But this yuletide some considered with concern,

That the fat man in a sleigh might be delayed in turn,

Not by fog, snow, sleet, muck, or murk,

But by a mountain of endless paperwork.

2 0 1 1

Mechanical Difficulties

'T was the very night before Christmas,

When Santa's sleigh broke down,

Without warning, without a spark,

Without a single grinding sound.

He looked at it for a long moment,

Wondering just what there was to fix,

But kicking it didn't help,

And shouting just left him in fits.

"I told you to get it serviced"

Said Rudolph, in tones most smug.

"But did you listen, of course not,

Just ignored it all with a shrug."

"It's not my fault," retorted Santa,

Most thoroughly and completely
displeased.

"The budget was spent on fog-lights,

Safety-features, and anti-pollution
shields.

With all the extras installed on board

There's hardly any room for toys anymore,

Especially with your mid-flight snack trough,

Taking up more than half the floor!

And it doesn't help that every year

There's always so much to dodge and weave,

Whether missiles fired in no-fly zones,

Or flocks of carelessly migrating geese.

Why it took me six weeks last year

To get the feathers out of the frame,

And the complaints from the animal lobby,

Have all but completely blackened my name."

He scratched his head most thoroughly,

And wondered who in the world to call,

For sleigh repair as a business,

Had been the first victim of Iceland's fall.

And he couldn't even begin to rely

On his elves' mechanical charms.

On hearing about the ice-caps melting,

Most had left the North Pole in alarm.

The few that remained in the workshop

Were now on a rather extended leave.

They were going to be extras in the Hobbit,

They said, and were busy reshooting scenes.

He considered using the social Internet,

To see what secrets might be had online.

But there he ran into a few roadblocks,

And one rather oversized mine.

"They've deactivated my Facebook account,"

He grumbled. "They're calling me a fake."

"And even the twitter people have twittered back,

Saying - "Be honest for goodness sake!""

With the online disbelief of Santa,

Fresh on his rather troubled mind,

He turned to the phone directory

Hoping for 'sleigh repair' to find.

The first number was engaged,

And the second was no longer in use,

The third number now sold flowers,

And the fourth responder was quite obtuse.

"Flying Sleighs?" they asked,

With a doubtfully dubious snort.

"We have Volkswagens and Fiats,

And various cars of every sort.

But tell us more about your sleigh,

And we will see about these complications."

So with little choice but to comply,

He gave them the technical specifications.

"Magic," they said with modest disapproval,

"Is no longer considered a clean energy source.

Try solar, wind, hydrogen or even ethanol,

Each and every one a renewable resource.

And the design, quite frankly,

Is far from aerodynamically sound,

Why, it's no wonder your reindeer

Complain of backaches all year round.

We recommend a newer model,

Something closer to the ground,

Perhaps a hovercraft, an ATV, or a VTOL

(though that isn't environmentally sound)."

"That's all well and good," grumbled Santa,

"But for Christmas, I need this sleigh.

It stops time, goes faster than light,

And leaves Einstein spinning in his grave.

It's the only way to get all these gifts

Delivered within the space of one single night,

Which, honestly, is a very unreasonable demand,

And one that my lawyer is trying to fight."

After a lengthy conversation and many an idea,

They referred Santa to the supercollidor crew,

Whose sole purpose was to upturn physics,

Destroy the world, or a combination of the two.

"No offence, old chap," they said to Santa,

"But you're simply too big for hyperlight
velocity.

You need to be small, smaller than an
atom,

As small as small can possibly ever be."

In the face of such negativity,

Santa decided to take a moment or three

To reflect solely on whether or not

Christmas was really worth this anarchy.

With a sigh he hung up on the scientists,

And on his defunct sleigh, he took his seat,

When Rudolph helpfully said, "Cheer up, boss,

If all else fails, we still have out feet."

So this Christmas if all gifts are late,

Take careful note of the reason why and heed,

Because no matter where you are in this world,

From the North Pole, it is a long walk indeed.

2 0 1 2

The Rant Before Christmas

’T was four nights before Christmas,

And the world had stubbornly refused to end,

Much to Santa's great disappointment,

Who'd seen the apocalypse as a godsend.

He paced and marched and huffed aloud,

Burdened as he was by problems galore,

Manufacturing, transport, animal welfare,

A thousand types of legislation and more.

This world's become too complicated,"

He declared, in tones most firm.

"Governments, and corporations, and armies

Enough to make a man squirm.

And bureaucracy lies all around me

No matter which direction I turn.

Mountains and mountains of documents,

I really can't help but want to burn.

I've submitted flight plans, and
visa requests,

And all sorts of other stuff,

But no matter how much
paperwork I provide

It never seems to be enough.

Midnight is a hectic time

On Christmas Eve, they say,

There's too much happening in the world

To worry about one flying sleigh.

Deliver your presents by Fedex,

Is the advice that I helpfully get.

No matter that the cost of such,

Would put me irreversibly in debt.

Not to mention the toys, which honestly,

Have become a veritable thorn in my side,

Patent laws mean I can't manufacture goods,

Without being accused of industrial homicide.

It's theft they do sternly declare,

Giving away what's sold on shelves,

Not to mention that most toy-makers

Refuse to outsource to elves."

Rudolph listened to all of this,

Bobbing his head and lazily cleaning his teeth,

Ever since Santa's therapist had quit,

These rants had been coming in twos and threes.

Personally, he was feeling quite content

To see Yuletide as a reasonably jolly time.

After all, for the bright-nosed reindeer,

It was (literally) his chance to shine.

And ever since visiting a friendly geneticist,

He'd got the nose light redone with themes,

It now blinked Morse code, dimmed on order,

And could shift from red to blue to green.

"Look, Boss," he said in a reasonable tone,

"It's the modern world, you see.

There's absolutely nothing that can be done

About its vast complexity.

But think of all those happy children.

I'm sure that'll make you smile.

Or at least," he added to himself,

"Make you stop fussing for a while."

"Ha," said Santa, even more depressed.

"Let me tell you about those kids,

Absolute monsters the lot of them,

Even the ones that don't tell fibs.

Last year they left traps waiting

Under half a dozen chimneys and trees,

Some were harmless, some were lethal,

And nearly all were infested with fleas.

Their lists get longer every single year,

And their arguments of morality are most precise,

This entire Christmas affair, they say,

Can no longer be simply a matter of naughty or nice.

And where once they used to leave snacks for me at night,

Cookies, a glass of milk, and the occasional jam tart,

Now I get a digestive biscuit and a note that says

'Dear Santa - We hope obesity doesn't stop your heart.'

Their concern might be considered touching,

When everything has been said and told,

But, honestly, that kind of talk,

Just makes me feel very, very old."

After that Santa continued

His lament in increasing detail

Particularly his conflict with

The world of sales and retail.

Seeing no options, Rudolph sighed and listened on,

Giving up on this red and white cloud of doom.

At the least, he supposed, complaining like this

Helped his boss's mind from going boom.

So if, during this Christmas, you happen to hear

A consistent grumpy muttering in the middle of the night,

Know that the bad news hasn't defeated Santa yet,

And that for better or worse - he's still in the fight.

2 0 1 3

The Accident Before Christmas

’T was three days before Christmas,

When Santa happened to break his leg,

An embarrassing incident really,

Since it happened while getting out of bed.

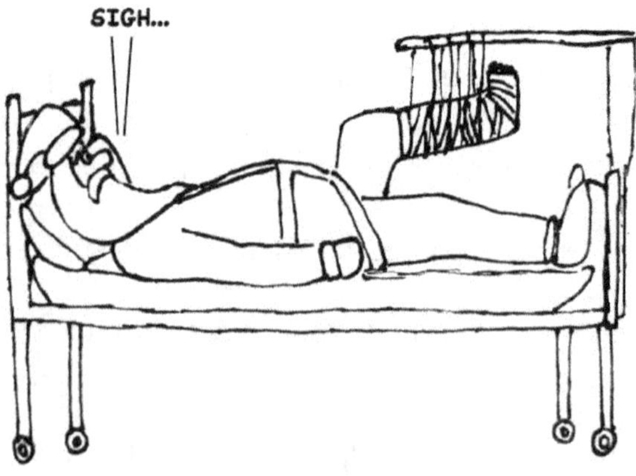

"I can tap dance on icy rooftops,"

He grumbled deep into his beard.

"And skate on the edge of chimneys,

Without any reason to be afeard.

But early in the morning with

A single carpet fold out of place,

And before I even know it,

There I am, lying flat on my face.

And the only elf qualified to fix this

Quit last month to follow his dreams.

Went off to fight some odd necromancer,

Or so, at least, it seems."

He glared balefully at his oversized cast,

And fretted about the most immediate
issue.

Who was going to do the work on
Christmas?

He really had absolutely no clue.

"It can't be the elves," he stated out loud.

"Get them to a chimney and all they do is wheeze.

All that soot and smoke and ash

Sets off all of their urban allergies.

It also can't be the reindeer,

They're great for flying and showing off
for the fans,

But when it comes to delivering presents,

Nothing beats the nimble work of a pair
of hands."

Still fretting most ardently,

Santa picked up his phone,

Looked through his contacts, dialled,

And waited for the ring tone.

The Sandman was unfortunately out

Negotiating his various movie rights.

The Easter Bunny was vacationing on Easter Island,

And apparently getting into lots of fights.

One by one, his choices slowly narrowed.

"This is disastrous," he said with a bellow.

"Why, things haven't been this bad since that

Halloween business with that Skellington fellow."

It was right around this moment

That Rudolph decided to speak up.

(He'd been skulking next to the doorway

Rather reluctant to interrupt)

"What about that backup?" he asked.

"That Santa Robot you had those
scientists make?

I thought it was ready to be tested,

Or did the artificial 'ho-ho-ho' prove
to be too fake?

At this, Santa let out an even larger sigh.

"It was perfect," he said, and threw up his hands.

"But then Google bought out the company

As part of their world domination plans."

"I guess there's nothing for it then,"

Said Rudolph with a most rueful grin,

And went off to fetch poor Santa crutches,

Some painkillers, and a bottle of gin.

So if this Christmas you happen to spot,

An awkward hobbling figure beside a sleigh upon a rooftop,

Do your best and give him a hand. After all,

At Christmas time, he's the one man who can't close shop.

2 0 1 4

Reindeer Escape

’T was two nights before Christmas,

And Santa had ended up in jail.

A most embarrassing incident, really,

Especially since they denied him bail.

"You're a flight risk," said the officer,

"It's right here in the lore.

Red suit, bushy beard, flying sleigh,

All those details and more.

Just sit tight and if all is well,

There's no reason you should have to be late,

Though we are having a little difficulty

Contacting the North Pole Consulate."

"That's because it's run by elves,"

Said Santa with the utmost despondency.

"Great at making toys and slaying orcs.

Not so good when it comes to diplomacy.

But, come, can't we just this once,

Perhaps look the other way?

It was a parking violation after all,

Not a murder on the highway."

"You're licensed," said the officer,

"For rooftops and for rooftops alone."

"But there you were just hovering around,

Less than ten feet from a telephone pole.

Could have tangled your reindeer in the lines,

And then what would you have to say?

As it is we've already had to report

This entire incident to the SPCA."

"It was an experiment," grumbled Santa.

"The new fad is delivering through a wall.

Over the years I've inhaled so much soot,

It's a wonder that I have any lungs left at all.

Not to mention that most children

No longer have chimneys in their homes.

Why, by next century I'll have to plan

To deliver to Mars and habitation domes.

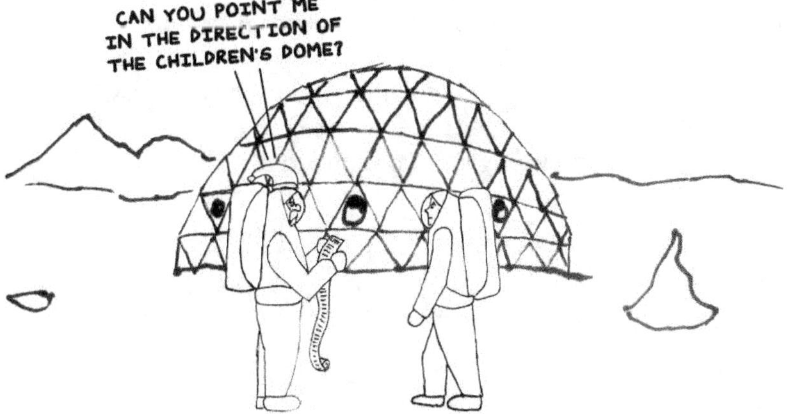

But the reindeer were perfectly safe.

Even when not flying or landing on a roof,

They are really quite agile,

And extraordinarily nimble of hoof.

And don't get me started on their treatment plan,

It's enough to drive a chap perfectly mental.

They have paid vacations, spa treatments,

Full health insurance, and even dental.

And now with all these hurricanes,

And snowstorms and rainstorms galore,

I've had them fitted for Magic Waterproof coats,

Which cost more than my entire workshop floor!

Where did you put them, by the way?

I do hope they aren't making too much of a fuss.

If they do get out of hand, remember,

Taking away their television privileges is a must."

"They're at a local wildlife sanctuary,"

Said the officer, taking note of the time.

"But I have to write the case up now,

Hopefully it should only be a small fine."

Santa watched the officer go,

Thinking gloomily about legal fees,

And about his other outstanding warrants,

From at least fifteen other countries.

He'd done his very best, honestly,

In his long years as Santa Claus,

But it's hard to deliver presents to millions,

Without breaking more than a few laws.

Toy manufacturing and copyright infringement,

And passing moral judgment on minors was bad enough,

But then people tended to bring up religion...

As if children cared why they got presents and stuff.

Despairing of spending years more in jail,

Santa sighed, and sat back in his cell,

Only to hear a soft snuffling,

And the ringing of a very small bell.

From outside the small window,

Covered securely with a series of bars,

A bright red light shone in,

Blotting out the evening stars.

"Hey Boss," said the one and only Rudolph,

Staring in with a well-kept smile.

"You look like you've had enough,

Of prison cells for a while."

For a long moment, Santa stared back,

Before spluttering in surprise.

"I thought you lot were in a sanctuary,

Fenced safely away from prying eyes."

"Wasn't for us," said Rudolph,

"Barbaric the whole place was,

"No TV, no grooming, no soft beds,

And not a single strand of dental floss.

Dangerous too," he added darkly.

"Wolves, mountain lions, and even a bear, no fear!

Why even the snooty Elks strut about,

Looking down on us fine specimens of reindeer."

So a rope was quietly slipped in,

And looped tightly around the window bars,

No match for a group of reindeer,

Destined to fly all the way to Mars.

So, this Christmas if Santa's laughter is hushed,

And he creeps about quietly during his yuletide call,

You have to understand his sense of caution.

For the moment, he is a wanted man, after all.

2015

An Invisible Christmas

'T was a week before Christmas,

When Santa received a letter.

Not unusual for this time of the year,

But the news could have been better.

The envelope was of the traditional mould,

Red and green trimming most bonafide,

Yet when he slit it open,

No child's wishlist lay inside.

Instead a note from his travel agent,

Which Santa read and then sighed.

Not only had the agent given notice,

But nineteen pending visas had been denied.

"Well, that's a blow, to be sure,"

He muttered to his chief clerk.

A tall elf with an intellectual air,

And an annoyingly sarcastic smirk.

"What did you really expect?"

Asked the elf, reading the note left there.

"With your history of customs violations,

It's a wonder that you're allowed anywhere.

And you've trespassed in air corridors,

No-fly zones, and even that one time

You interrupted that space shuttle launch,

And they gave you that hefty fine."

"Flying a sleigh these days is complicated,"

Said Santa with a wearied sort of groan.

"Never mind the planes and helicopters,

The other day I hit a delivery drone.

And as for those bureaucrats in customs,

They're all really quite unreasonable.

They don't understand that searching

Every present just isn't feasible.

Even though I have the permits,

And monthly inspections through the year,

Some bureaucrats don't seem to get,

That Christmas toys are not something to fear.

And then they try and levy duties and taxes

On every present that I should happen to bear,

Which would cost me more than the whole North Pole.

As if my accounts weren't already a nightmare.

And there was the animal smuggling charge,

Relating to Rudolph and the rest.

Even though they each had flight permits,

And were just trying to do their best.

But now they've just sealed their borders,

Claiming it's for reasons of security.

They say this Christmas business is odd,

Despite my reputation for honesty.

I've half a mind to go on strike,

And let someone else do the work.

Let them brave the night-time
pollution,

Breathing in the smog, the smoke, and
the murk.

It's taken years off my rather elongated life,

And the dangers of the job are growing with each passing night.

First it was NORAD fighter jets tailing me,

And now in Somalia, I can even be legally shot on sight.

I'd like to see someone else,

Manage all this responsibility.

It's become so much more,

Than simple holiday festivity.

No longer do I have to consider,

Mere questions of naughty and nice,

But whether or not children have food,

Are healthy, or free of lice.

Forget the simple days of responding to personal requests,

Of hovering over chimneys with warm fires inside,

Now it's a matter of tracking families across continents,

And trying to deliver cheer to people who have to hide."

MAYBE NEXT TIME, FEWER TOYS, MORE BLANKETS?

Grumbling darkly and continually to himself,

Santa seemed quite keen on his plan.

He got to his feet intending to implement

His acceptance of a worldwide Christmas ban.

Then out of nowhere, seemingly,

Appeared Rudolph out of thin air.

Giving both the not-so-jolly fat man,

And the intellectual elf quite a scare.

"Did you see that, Boss?" asked the reindeer,

With completely undisguised glee.
"The elves in the tech department worked this out

To help with your immigration difficulty."

He flicked his eyes to a device,

Resting snugly atop his head.

It was small, metallic looking,

With lights blinking blue and red.

"Personal cloaking devices," declared Rudolph.

"One for each reindeer and one for the sleigh.

All personally guaranteed to keep fighter jets,

And bureaucratic border officials at bay.

So for once, let's just ignore the paperwork,

And do the job because it's worthwhile?"

Santa stared at him long and hard,

And then slowly, he started to smile.

So this year if you don't see Santa, you know why.

For those protective of borders should beware,

When it comes to restrictions born of fear,

An invisible Santa really doesn't care.

2 0 1 6

The Surrender of Santa

’T was three weeks before Christmas,

And Santa was in a bit of a mood,

To be expected, it might be said,

Since he was being unexpectedly sued.

"It's like this," said his lawyer,

In tones self-important and verbose,

(Online schools had given Rudolph

A degree along with his shining nose)

"It's this whole nationalism business

That's gotten just a tiny bit out of hand.

So a bunch of nations are making this

Strange and rather unreasonable demand.

'Christmas is all well and good', they say,

'Fly where you will with your sleigh and toy bag,

But if you do enter our airspace,

You are now required to fly that country's flag.'"

Santa's beard twitched in quiet fury,

As he gave his reindeer lawyer a frown.

"Say what you will," said Rudolph defensively.

"It's a sight better than being shot down.

We can argue it legally, of course,

And try and have the suit overturned.

But it's their courts that make the rules,

And it's very easy to get burned.

Besides, it can be rather awkward,

And I prefer to be circumspect,

For in the human legal system,

Talking reindeers get no respect."

"Isn't it enough," growled Santa,

A deep weariness evident in his tone,

"That they tie me up in red tape,

And expect me to work myself to the bone.

With all they've done with this planet,

They've all but ruined my home,

For every summer now I'm forced

To live inside an undersea dome.

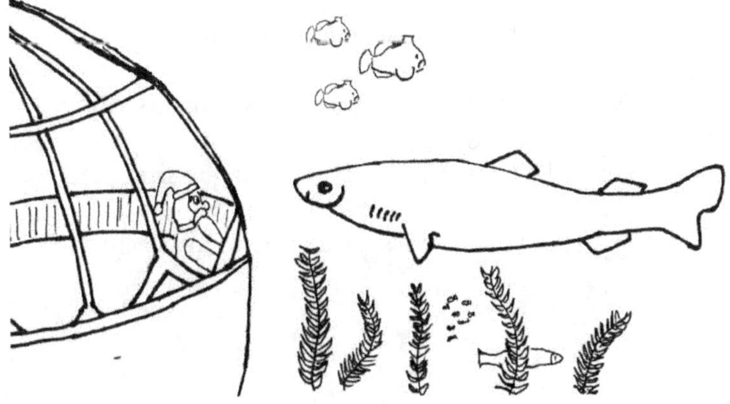

The refitting and remodelling of the workshop

Was a complete and total nightmare.

And the elves certainly weren't happy about it

(Though they never are, to be fair).

It's not like they can move to another country,

What with this wave of anti-immigration fears.

Despite all this talk about equality and tolerance,

There are always those who frown at pointy ears.

But melting of Arctic ice aside,

The problems that I've had to go through!

I could go on and on about them,

Till my face turns a vivid shade of blue!

From the Earth's magnetic field weakening,

And sending my navigational instruments astray,

To all the reindeers shrinking in size,

And smartphones setting fire to my sleigh!

I have to fly low now, to avoid air traffic,

Birds, helicopters, planes, drones and all.

But now I can't fly from one country to the next,

Without worrying about hitting a wall!

I've modernized and revolutionized

To keep pace with change and try not to fail.

Did you know that most kids today

Refuse to send letters that aren't e-mail?

The tech elves now have algorithms,

For sorting out the naughty and nice,

And all I can do is hover in the background,

And pretend to give sound advice.

And the letters themselves are enough,

To rob this Christmas spirit of good cheer,

Where once was hope and innocence,

Now lies a future filled with fear.

And it seems to me, but this whole economy thing,

Has some governments being really far too rash.

In India, Venezuela, and other countries as well,

Instead of presents, children are asking for cash!

And even in places like the United Kingdom,

Where I was once received with joy and elation,

Now they won't even authorize my flight plans,

Until they know my views on the European nation.

No, I say," said Santa firmly,

"Even if it is supposed to be a law,

This entire flag business is

Totally and completely the last straw."

"All right," said Rudolph quickly,

Still cheerful in the face of this tirade.

"We do have some other options,

And there's a strong case here to be made.

We can organize a protest perhaps,

Or if all else should fail,

Then we can say the legal notice,

Just got lost in the mail.

And in the meantime, I've got an idea,

For getting through this Christmas intact.

It's a brilliant idea, in my opinion,

One that combines both cunning and tact."

So Santa listened, with a skeptical air,

To the not-so-humble reindeer's master plan.

And finally agreed with a "Why not?

I guess this is doing the best that we can."

So on this year's Christmas,

Some might happen to spy

A glimpse of Santa's sleigh,

And the flag that he's chosen to fly.

Pale as snow

And plain as night,

Symbolic and devious,

Perfectly white.

Representing the Arctic, a protest, and a surrender of sorts,

As he flies over cities and forests of elm and spruce,

Know that between all the nations of the world and Santa,

There is, for this one yuletide night at least, a truce.

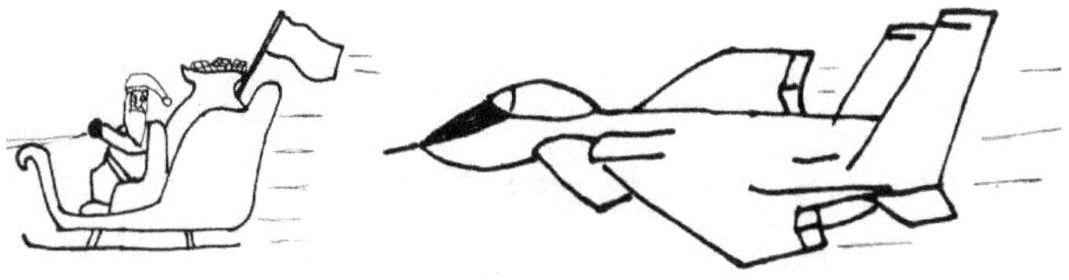

2 0 1 7

The Tale of Whitebeard

'T was a week and a half before Christmas,

And Santa appeared lost at sea,

While some might take this is a metaphor,

This was meant quite literally.

He'd been missing for three days now,

After testing out his new amphibious sleigh.

(What with rising water levels all around

He knew he had to be prepared for the day)

In his absence, Rudolph took charge,

Conducting the search, and keeping everyone in the know.

Transparency was very important to him;

He didn't want anyone mistaking this for a coup or an overthrow.

The Arctic listening posts were activated,

And the search teams of polar bears and seals organized one-by-one,

(There were not as many as Rudolph would have liked,

They were fast becoming endangered by a little too much heat and sun)

He even called up the penguins,

All the way on the other side of the world,

Who were rather rude and unhelpful,

And said: "If he were here, we would have heard."

It was finally a narwhal that found him,

While swimming swiftly through the frigid Arctic sea,

"There's a problem," came the message to Rudolph.

"The sleigh's still afloat, but he says to leave him be.

He's had it with Christmas, he says,

And believes the sleigh's breakdown to be a sign,

A perfect excuse to take the year off,

To simply float around on the currents and whine."

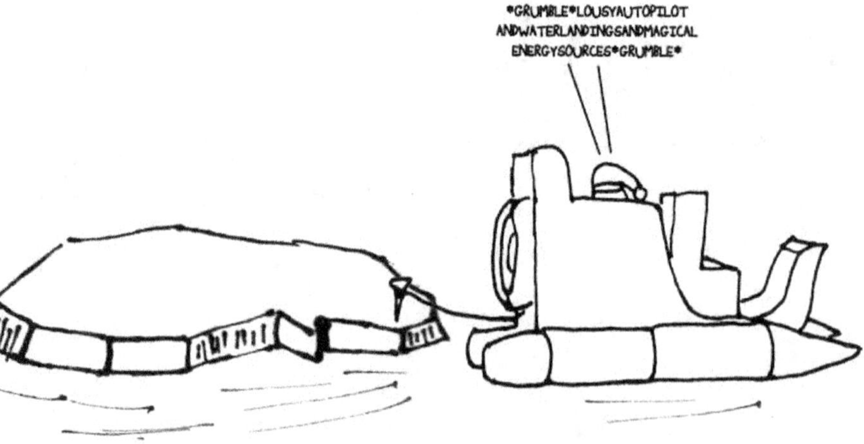

"Honestly," groaned Rudolph, shaking his horns,

And swiftly and speedily taking to the clear blue skies,

"The amount of maintenance this boss takes -

The new ideas, the therapy, the freshly baked pork pies!

His misanthropy is getting worse with every year.

It's almost more trouble than it's worth.

I have to keep reminding him it's for the children,

And the need to create joy and mirth."

Still Rudolph was relieved, even as he complained,

Speeding faster through the sky than a bat out of hell,

The fact that Santa was grumbling and groaning,

Was a perfectly good sign that he was alive and well.

He finally reached the amphibious sleigh,

Now parked and anchored near a lonely ice floe,

Rudolph flashed his nasal landing light,

And finally cooled his hooves in the snow.

"Time to go to work, Boss,"

He said firmly, but with a good dose of cheer,

"Let's get this sleigh all fixed up,

And load it up for Christmas this year."

"I really can't see what the point of it all is,"

Said Santa, turning and grumpily glaring at the reindeer.

"It's a far better way to spend Christmas floating,

Than plunge back into the world with all its hate and fear.

I really thought things were getting better,

What with technology and awareness, and basic human rights,

But suddenly people who miss the dark ages are

Coming out of the woodwork and getting into ridiculous fights.

You'd think with all that humans have to attend,

Between hurricanes and earthquakes and wildfires galore,

They wouldn't have time for pettiness and bickering,

But instead there's nationalism, sexism, racism, and more!

Christmas delivery is impossible if you think about it.

Every year I've delivered to all from east to west,

But I'm told that I can't visit certain countries anymore,

Without putting some inane travel ban to the test.

I don't even know how many nations there are on any given day.

Between referendums and invasions, and actual civil war.

None of this politicking nonsense and neighbourly strife,

Was written anywhere in the original Christmas lore.

I've generally tried to stay absolutely neutral,

To religion, ideology, country, or creed.

To celebrate a day with presents and warmth,

And a momentary absence of any greed.

Though there really is a war on me and Christmas," he said darkly,

"My summer home is in ruins, falling through melting ice into a hole.

But when I try and get someone to listen and do something about it,

They ignore me completely, and these idiots just keep on burning coal!

And then they make arguments about who exactly I am,

Their fixation on me being old, white, and fat is tragic,

Through the years I've been every age, weight, and skin colour.

Don't they understand - it's all part of being magic!

Honestly, if belief allowed, I'd be a woman next year,"

He said with a despairing sort of sigh,

"Christmas might be better," he said, "And after all,

If the Doctor can do it, why can't I?"

"I'm all for it, boss," said Rudolph,

Fixing the sleigh with both exasperation and amused glee.

Letting Santa rant as he worked,

Was his very own version of yuletide psychotherapy.

"But you've got to keep your hopes up, boss,"

He said, his furry face beaming with a slighlty forced smile

"Every Christmas we improve in small but significant ways,

We talk, argue and make things better by an inch or a mile.

And everyone who dreams of better days,

Sometimes only needs a sort of sample,

Of fairness, equality, and kindness,

And your workshop is a good example.

We've always had equal hiring on the species front,

Goblins, gnomes, elves, of every colour and nationality,

(Though preventing genocide on the workshop floor,

Has become an unfortunately necessary speciality.)

We've had equal pay for all genders for two centuries now,

Though, yes, there are still some things that need fixing,

But look how things like reindeer morale have improved,

Especially since you fired Dancer for harassing Blitzen.

Now, I understand Christmas is stressful for you,

It's nonstop work, while always being on the run,

But I've got a great idea of how to make things interesting,

To skirt around human politics and really have fun."

So Santa listened carefully to Rudolph's plan,

While the sleigh hummed and roared back to life,

And started cruising through the water,

On a voyage for Christmas, circumventing strife.

Santa was equipped with an eye-patch, a parrot,

And a crew for his now seaworthy sleigh/boat,

And cannons to fire presents very precisely from

International waters, where he can safely float.

So from ocean to ocean, drifting this Christmas night,

Beware of a new winter pirate, seeking not really to pillage,

But rather trying out innovative, new, and fun ways,

To rain presents and cheer down on every city, town, and village.

So this Christmas, if you hear the cannons roar,

And have to dodge well-padded presents fired from far away,

Know that things could be worse for Christmas,

And that, for now at least, we have Whitebeard and his sleigh.

2 0 1 8

The Noel Conspiracy

’Twas about four days before Christmas,

And Santa was hiding away under his bed,

That is to say - beneath the trapdoor that

Concealed his secret workshop and sleigh shed.

He was watching his many security monitors

With a paranoid gleam on his round and bearded face,

While setting out various items on a workbench,

Including a stun-gun, brass-knuckles and a can of mace.

He was mumbling and muttering to himself,

While drinking tea and trying to keep awake.

The last few weeks had been troubling,

And he was sure that he wasn't making a mistake.

"They're out to get me!" he declared,

In tones both sonorous and dramatic.

But then followed that by spilling some tea,

Which was honestly quite anticlimactic.

"Drones have been flying past for weeks now.

And there have been disturbances in the workshop.

And just three days ago, the head custodial elf

Said he had to chase away an intruder with a mop!

It's bad enough that I'm told

That in around twelve years I'll be out of a job,

What with the world we know ending

And humanity reduced to an angry and scared mob.

But do the countries of the world see the science,

Take note of the dangers and choose to act?

Or do they sit around for ages squabbling,

While declaring gut feelings as truth and fact?"

Santa drained his cup and set it aside,

Moving to one corner of his secret lair.

He rummaged through a pile of discarded toys,

Extracting a belt of tools that he kept there.

"This is all because of the petition I submitted,"

He muttered as his next steps he began to prepare.

"I tried to tell the UN about the arctic ice issues.

But they called me biased, which really isn't fair.

It's not just the workshop and my home

That I'm trying unsuccessfully to save.

But there's a whole Elven nation here,

Filled with people, both strange and brave.

Since then, I am absolutely, positively
certain,

(I'd swear to it by my favourite pair of
moccasins)

That certain unsavoury governments
of the world,

Have dispatched towards me - a squad
of assassins."

There was a sound from another corner,

A long sigh from the other occupant of the shed.

Rudolph yawned widely as he emerged from slumber,

He stood up, blinking his nose and raising his head.

He moved to stand quite strategically,

Between Santa and his trusted (if very temperamental) sleigh,

So that the old man couldn't follow through

On his plans to arm the vehicle to the teeth for Christmas Day.

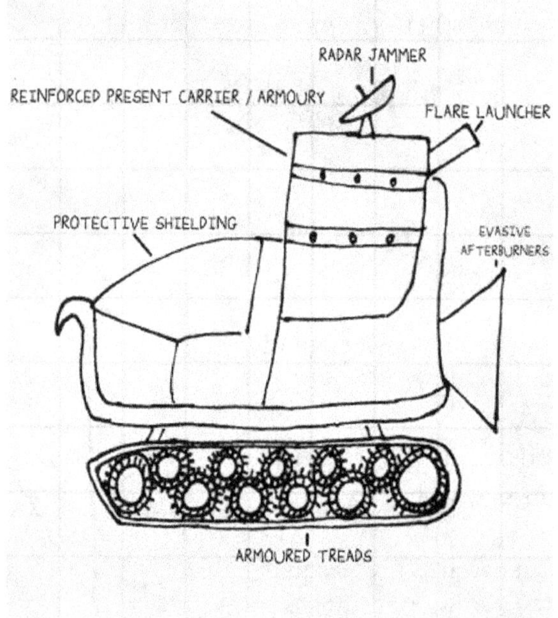

"You're just being paranoid,"

He said soothingly to calm the mood.

"You've been overworked, is all.

Just get some sleep and have some food."

"How can you say that?" grumbled Santa,

"Humanity has clearly gone all sorts of insane.

Between trade wars and actual wars,

And this nationalism disease affecting their brain.

It seems that they're trying to stop global warming,

With disagreements leading to a nuclear winter instead.

And they're no longer happy with green Christmas trees.

I have no idea what's happening in their collective head.

And the letters I've been getting,

Which normally fill me with joy and cheer,

Have been getting darker and stranger,

And it does not bode well for Christmas this
year.

I've had children by the thousands asking

If I could reunite them with their families,

Or asking if I can stop wars or save areas from

Floods, fires, and all sorts of calamities.

And some of these letters, I'd definitely swear,

Were absolutely not written by actual children at all.

Requests for polonium and bonesaws for example,

And this one apparent toddler who keeps asking for a wall.

Most governments see me as a Christmas trespasser -

An illegal alien to be shown swiftly to the exit door.

Though between political dysfunction and outright shutdowns,

I can slip through with them being none the wiser for."

"Come now. It's not all bad," said Rudolph,

Seeing that his boss was finally running out of steam.

"Even if they're all mad and out to get you,

We've got a job to do, protecting every hope and every dream.

Sure the world may be burning,

But at least they're all regularly talking about it now.

And some at least, aren't fighting,

But working to fix the problems and explaining the how.

Putting aside the sheer amount of chaos and insanity,

There are at least a handful or two of positive trends,

There's peace in the Koreas (though by accident, perhaps)

And in India, LGBTQ people can legally be more than friends.

In Japan, the borders are opening,

And they've even invited the elves to immigrate,

(Though what with their longevity,

I fear it may not really help their low birth rate)

Renewable energy is on a clear and increasing rise

And seems to finally be more than a fad,

And this whole crypto-currency mania seems to be done with.

Really, that nonsense was quite completely mad.

And while disaster has killed countless,

It has always been met with resolve quite brave,

And there was even that feel-good story,

When they got those kids in Thailand out of that cave.

Even in places such as the United States,

What with their recent reversion to the past,

Seems to have turned a sensible corner,

And at least started listening to women at last.

And even if all fails and civilization ends,"

Said Rudolph with a confident and slightly cocky smile.

"We change our business model to purely humanitarian aid,

And try to keep hope alive, even if just for a while."

"All right, all right," said Santa with exasperation,

Putting away his tools and plans for arming the sleigh.

"Even if it does mean risking my life and limb,

We'll continue on doing things the right and proper way.

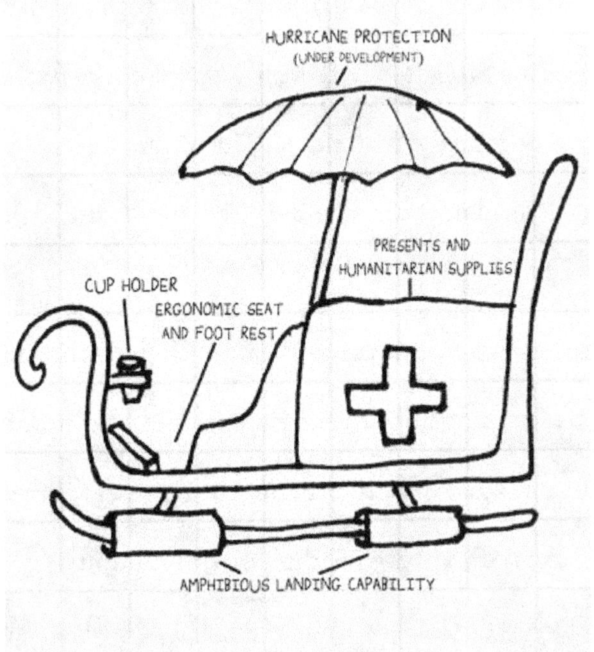

But that doesn't mean I won't be prepared,"

He went on with a gleam in his eye.

"Just because I'm supposed to cheerful and jolly,

Does not mean that I'm prepared to die."

So quickly and surely Santa laid out his plan,

While Rudolph listened to it all with a skeptical stare.

And so it was decided to bring in some help,

From the Elven Nation, whose space they happened to share.

So this Christmas, in a world filled with fear,

Hearken to sleigh-bells flying though the cool night,

Seemingly unafraid of hidden assassins,

And cloaked in a warm (and slightly hard to see) light.

Set out a welcome for Santa - the new Elven Ambassador,

Tasked to bring hope to every nation and community,

Clad in a mixture of optimism, mirth, cheer and above all,

A very hefty dose of diplomatic immunity.

2019

A Social Reindeer Story

’T was a few days or so before Christmas,

And Santa was hiding from a certain reindeer.

Though ordinarily a good friend and co-worker,

Lately, Rudolph had been a drain on holiday cheer.

Pacing amidst a never-ending labyrinth

Of toy packaging, manufacturing, and assembly lines,

Santa muttered to himself furtively,

While distractedly counting gifts by the nines.

"It all started when he went Social,"

Santa complained quietly to the world at large.

The nearest quality inspection elf

Rolled her eyes, trying to ignore the man in charge.

"First it was only stuff like Facebook,

Used to keep in touch with the penguins down south,

Then he joined Twitter, Instagram, Snapchat,

And other things that had him frothing at the mouth.

I knew from the start that this wouldn't end well.

Before he was joyfully tap-dancing from roof to roof,

But then he got it in his head to be modern,

And the team chipped in for a phone operated by hoof.

Only now do we see the consequences,

And the damage has already been done.

He's become paranoid, narcissistic,

And has really become a lot less fun.

He won't eat a meal without
photographing it first,

Even though his diet is mostly just
leaves and moss.

People have started believing he's a
botanist,

While he argues that any non-lichen
food is a loss.

And I do fear that being this connected,

Has really gone straight to his head.

A talking reindeer is bound to be popular,

Even without a nose that glows bright red.

He's been approached by the powers that be,

Corporations of every kind and every creed,

Wanted to place samples of their products,

In every nook and cranny of his social feed.

He claims that it's really all about self-expression,

Freedom of speech and all that stuff,

Though when China complained about his panda rant,

He took down the post quickly enough.

And the ideas he's been hearing about Christmas

Are really very worrying to say the least,

He thinks cyber-surveillance and big data can solve

The naughty and nice list from west to east.

I understand that it might in some ways be practical,

And possibly the most efficient way to get things done.

Yet it might land us on the wrong side of that list,

And besides - sometimes the older ways are more fun."

It was then that the very reindeer in question,

Peeked in with the forlorn look of a guilt-ridden thief.

The elf noticed, and jerked her head towards Santa,

Inwardly breathing a long and heavy sigh of relief.

Seeing that a conversation was in order,

Santa tried to stifle a loud and annoyed sniff.

He followed Rudolph to his office,

And then waited patiently with his beard held stiff.

"It's like this," started Rudolph apologetically,

"I know that being this connected hasn't been good.

But I'm convinced that there's a lot that we can do,

And even some things that we absolutely should.

Most years, you complain non-stop about the world,

Of chaos, fanaticism, corruption and strife.

Which I've started to really discover this year,

Amidst the complex wonder of everyday life.

I'll admit that I've gotten a little lost,

But I have some thoughts that I really want to share.

And I promise to really think them through.

None of that 'follow and retweet for presents' affair.

Besides, you've always talked about

The absolute necessity of change.

We've got to look at all the options

If we want Christmas to have more range.

Sure, while it's certainly not ideal

To tweet and shout into the endless Void,

Perhaps, instead, we could just listen,

And try not to get irrationally annoyed?

Right now, across countries the world over,

There are people trying to be heard.

And if authoritarian net blackouts continue

It may just be their very last word."

Santa considered all this with a ponderous silence,

While Rudolph nervously twitched his stubby tail.

"All right," said Santa with a hefty sigh.

"I daresay it can't be worse than Christmas email.

We do need to be involved,

And aware of what people really need.

That is certainly important,

When plotting one's next good deed.

We have to be prepared for all the calamities to come,

Between nationalist nonsense and baby Yoda memes,

To the growing range of climate change threats -

Fires, floods, blizzards and more extremes.

We certainly can't trust the humans to fix things,

Since most of their leaders just shout obscenities into their mic,

And the only ones to make any sense at all

Are complete odd-bods such as Swedish teenagers and the like."

So the two went to work on a yuletide social media plan,

To listen to the online pulse of the world as best they could,

And perhaps use the Internet as it had been intended -

To reach out, listen with open minds, and even do some good.

So this Christmas, if you do so happen to find

Yourself sharing or shouting into the endless digital world,

Know that you're not alone, and for better or worse,

There's at least one reindeer listening with ears unfurled.

EPILOGUE: 2020

The Once and Future Claus

’Twas an hour and a half before Christmas,

And I walked my workshop whilst deep in thought,

Unshaken by the chaos of years’ past;

Battles lost and won and yet to be fought.

What events we have all stood witness to,

Pains of a century’s adolescence

Once more haunting uncertain futures

As we sort between reason and nonsense.

The elves work hard till the very last hours,

Their gifts now for more than just girls and boys.

Year round, they've woven masks and gear for all,

Where once they only manufactured toys.

I watch their craftsmanship with deepest pride,

Allayed only by a fear at my core,

That future's folly may see their skill,

Turning darkly to make weapons of war.

Lost memories of what I used to be.

Of solstice and the winter king of old,

Of what came before all the mirth and joy,

Of what lay beneath, watching eons unfold.

And yet where once I was but a fable,

Something to beat back winter's undying fear,

Now I am among friends and family,

Ready as herald of the twelfth month's cheer.

Between bleak midwinter eve and spring's dawn,

There are lessons learnt with each new season.

Reindeer and sleigh await and my thoughts clear.

For this night, I have my work and reason.

To fly and laugh in the face of despair,

And to give to all those who cannot cope,

No alms richer than a touch of kindness,

And no gift greater than an ounce of hope.

THE END

About the Author

Kuber Kaushik was born in Calcutta, India and subsequently raised on a steady diet of Asimov, Tolkien, and Pratchett and his love for the written word has only grown stronger over time. He has been a blogger, copywriter, content writer, script writer, screenwriter, and novelist – crafting words and stories in various forms.

His first feature film script (Shadows Fall) was produced in 2016 and both screened and won awards at film festivals in Los Angeles, Panama, and Europe. His other works include a number of short-films, short stories, and even a comic strip chronicling 9000 years of healthcare and the insanity therein.

His debut novel – The Children of Destruction – was published in March 2019 by Penguin Random House India. He has finished his second manuscript – an urban fantasy novel, Demon's Pride, and is currently working on sequels to both books amid other projects.

His aim in story-telling has always been to bring colorful characters to life and explore and build new worlds with each story. He is currently represented by the Labyrinth Literary Agency (http://www.labyrinthagency.com) and can be found on twitter @thegingap.

Books By This Author

<u>The Children of Destruction</u>

For Alice, life as a teenager is hard enough without turning into a supernatural herald of destruction. And you would think that after causing minor hurricanes with a major sneeze, being visited by a talking fox and ending up on a journey with death around every corner, things can't get much worse.

Wrong.

They can.

Between a blind and telekinetic mass murderer, a girl bound to a shadow-demon and a genetically engineered pseudo messiah, a whole generation of weird is ready to come of age. And when it does, the world will change.

If it survives that long.